101 ways to BRUSH YOUR TEETH

Always supervise young children when they're brushing their teeth.

Imogen Foster   Tony Neal

HODDER

Big teeth, **sharp** teeth, **small** teeth,

smooth teeth, **wonky** teeth, and **chompy, chewy** teeth.

Teeth come in all shapes and sizes! We need our teeth for chewing and eating food, but if you don't look after them, they won't be all that nice.

Spiders have long, pointed fangs!

So, find a grown-up and don't forget to **brush your teeth!**

You can brush your teeth almost anywhere, doing almost **anything.**

Standing up,

sitting down,

with **crossed** legs,

stretched legs

or **very-tangled-up** legs.

On your **belly,**

on your knees,
on tippy **toes,**

on your
bum,

with one hand on your **head**

Flamingos don't have teeth at all.

and balancing on one leg. **Keeeeep still!**

Walking, **talking,**

hopping, skipping, **jumping,**

stomping,

strutting,

slouching,

and marching
in a line!

Tiny ants have tinier teeth –
and they're very strong!

Happy brushing,

grumpy brushing,

sleepy brushing,

sulky brushing

and **little-bit-sneezy** brushing. (ACHOOOO!)

Quick brushing,

Slooooooow... brushing ...

Snails have more teeth than any animal – they can have over 25,000!

and when you're in a **rush** brushing.

You can brush all around the **house.**

In the **bed,**

under the **bed,**

on the **table,** on the **chairs**

and up the **stairs.**

To the **shower**, to the **bath**

and on the **loo . . .**

but **NOT** when you're doing a poo! **Ew!**

Brush in the **sink**

Lobsters and crabs have teeth in their stomachs!

and **in places you wouldn't think.**

Pretend to brush in **faraway lands**.

Like a **knight**,
or a **queen**,

or a **wizard**
with a wand,

on a **magic carpet** and even on an old **witch's broom.**

With your **eyes closed,**

or **WIDE open,**

Adult grey wolves have 42 teeth. Adult humans only have 32.

wearing **slippers** or someone else's **pyjamas!**

Imagine a **jungle** where everyone's brushing.

Brush **big** like a bonobo, or **purring** like a panther,

Saltwater crocodiles have the strongest BITE!

lounging like a lizard,

and **creeping** like a crocodile.

Brush **grinning** like a gorilla,

laughing like a lemur,

and show off those **terrible tiger teeth.**

Biting,

singing,

slithering,

A snake's teeth are filled with venom, which can be poisonous.

swinging and **hanging upside down.**

And up in **space**, astronauts brush too.

Pulling, **pushing,**

working,

fixing, and **taking in the view.**

Floating,

somersaulting,

spacewalking,

It's very difficult to brush your teeth in space – you have to stop your toothbrush from floating away!

and **bouncing on the moon! Wahooo!**

And back on Earth, you can brush **AND** do sports.

Yoga brushing,

scooter brushing,

skateboard brushing,

Cows have very busy teeth – they chew for eight hours a day!

and **balancing-on-your-bike** brushing.

Football brushing,

ballet brushing,

kung-fu brushing,

and **twirling round and round** brushing. **Weeeee!**

And then there are the days when you're just too tired for brushing adventures.

So, brush with your **mum,** your **dad,**

your **brother,** your **sister** and the **baby** too.

Invite **granny** and **grandad**,

a **friend**

and help your **teddy** brush his pegs with you.

From bottom to top, your teeth to your tongue, when brushing twice daily **you can't go wrong!**

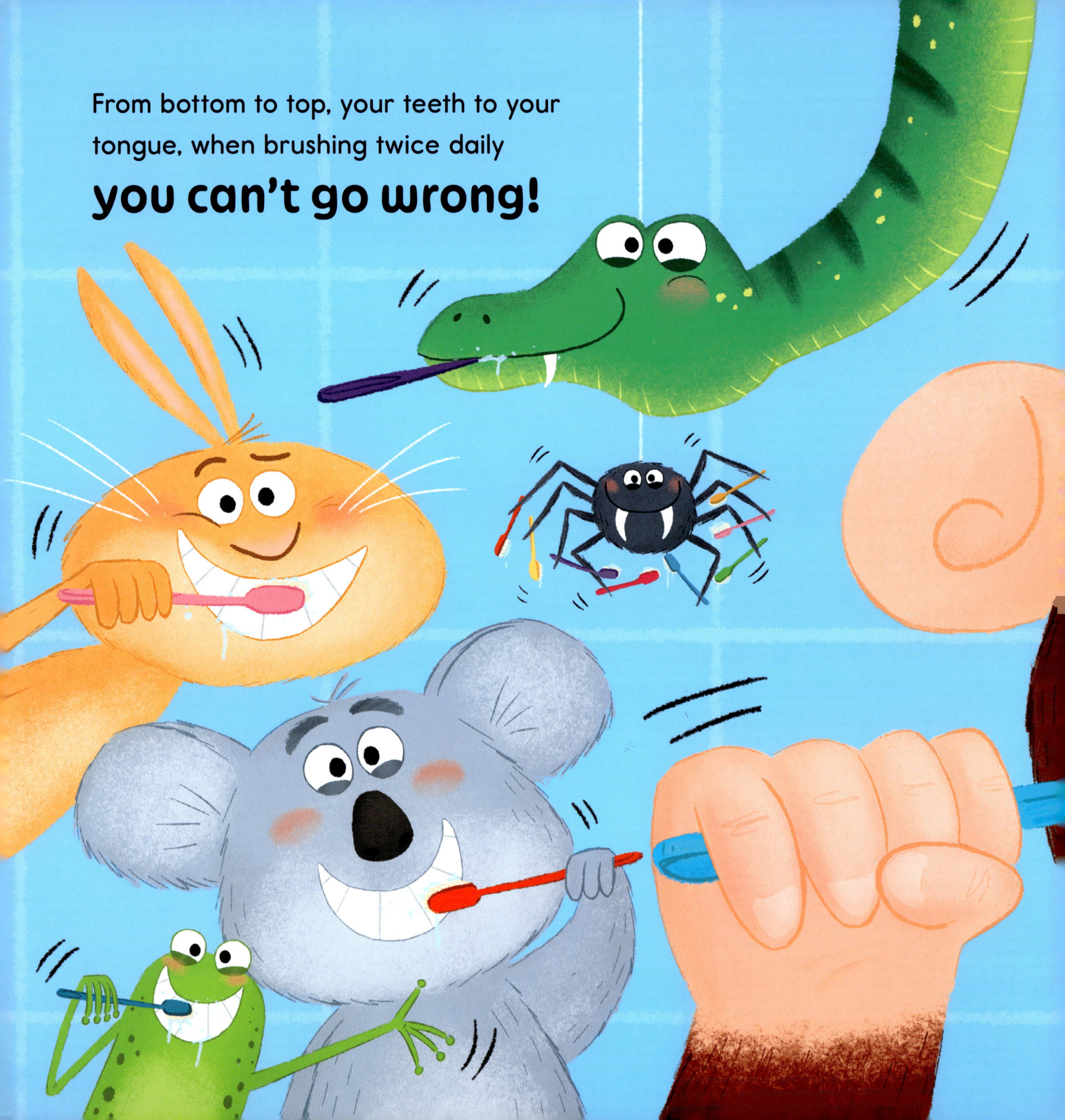

There are **101 ways** to brush your teeth in this book. How many can **YOU** try?

Why is it important to
brush your teeth?

- Brushing your teeth helps keep them **clean and healthy.** It gets rid of leftover food that might be stuck between them and whips away any **nasty germs.**

- If we don't brush, then our teeth and gums can get infected or feel sore. Your teeth might start to rot, and they could even **fall out!**

- Brushing also helps stop your breath from getting **stinky.**

Top tips for **terrific** teeth brushing

- Remember to brush your teeth **two** times every day – in the morning and before you go to bed at night.

- Choose a **toothbrush** that you love. It could be blue, pink or even sparkly.

- Squeeze your toothpaste carefully onto your brush. You need a **blob** about the size of a pea.

- Brush your teeth for **two minutes.** Make sure you get every tooth, from your bottom ones to your top ones. **And don't forget to brush your tongue, too!**

- Try brushing in front of a **mirror** so you can see where your brush is cleaning.

- Brush your teeth with a grown-up's help.

- If you remember to do all these things, then your teeth will be **shiny and healthy!**

To teeth everywhere,
beware of popcorn kernels

I.F.

For Olive

T.N.

HODDER CHILDREN'S BOOKS
First published in Great Britain in 2025
by Hodder and Stoughton

1 3 5 7 9 10 8 6 4 2

Copyright © Hodder and Stoughton Limited, 2025
Illustrations by Tony Neal

PB ISBN 978-1-44497-292-4
E-book ISBN 978-1-44497-810-0

Printed in China

FSC
www.fsc.org

MIX
Paper | Supporting
responsible forestry
FSC® C104740

Hodder Children's Books

An imprint of Hachette Group
Part of Hodder and Stoughton Limited
Carmelite House
50 Victoria Embankment
London, EC4Y 0DZ

An Hachette UK Company
www.hachette.co.uk
www.hachettechildrens.co.uk

The authorised representative in the EEA is
Hachette Ireland, 8 Castlecourt Centre, Dublin 15,
D15 XTP3, Ireland (email: info@hbgi.ie)